D0813024

13 5 7 9 10 8 6 4 2

Vintage
20 Vauxhall Bridge Road,
London SW1V 2SA

Vintage Classics is part of the Penguin Random House
group of companies whose addresses can be found at
global.penguinrandomhouse.com.

 Penguin
Random House
UK

First published in Great Britain by Chatto & Windus in 2007
This short edition published by Vintage in 2017

penguin.co.uk/vintage

A CIP catalogue record for this book is available from the British Library

ISBN 9781784872700

Typeset in 9.5/14.5 pt FreightText Pro
by Jouve (UK), Milton Keynes
Printed and bound by Clays Ltd, St Ives plc

Penguin Random House is committed to a sustainable future for
our business, our readers and our planet. This book is made from
Forest Stewardship Council® certified paper.

MIX
Paper from
responsible sources
FSC® C018179

Language

XIAOLU GUO

VINTAGE MINIS

Before

Sorry of my english

prologue

prologue *n* introduction to a play or book

Now.

Beijing time 12 clock midnight.

London time 5 clock afternoon.

But I at neither time zone. I on airplane. Sitting on 25,000 km above to earth and trying remember all English I learning in school.

I not met you yet. You in future.

Looking outside the massive sky. Thinking air staffs need to set a special time-zone for long-distance airplanes, or passengers like me very confusing about time. When a body floating in air, which country she belonging to?

People's Republic of China passport bending in my pocket.

Passport type	P
Passport No.	G00350124
Name in full	Zhuang Xiao Qiao
Sex	Female
Date of birth	23 JULY 1979
Place of birth	Zhe Jiang, P. R. China

I worry bending passport bring trouble to immigration officer, he might doubting passport is fake and refusing me into the UK, even with noble word on the page:

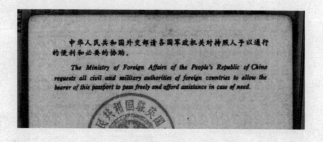

China further and further, disappearing behind clouds. Below is ocean. I from desert town. Is the first time my life I see sea. It look like a dream.

As I far away from China, I asking me why I coming to West. Why I must to study English like parents wish? Why I must to get diploma from West? I not knowing what I needing. Sometimes I not even caring what I needing. I not caring if I speaking English or not. Mother only speaking in village dialect and even not speaking official Mandarin, but she becoming rich with my father, from making shoes in our little town. Life OK. Why they want changing my life?

And how I living in strange country West alone? I never been to West. Only Western I seeing is man working in Beijing British Embassy behind tiny window. He stamp visa on brand new passport.

What else I knowing about West? American TV series dubbing into Chinese, showing us big houses in suburb, wife by window cooking and car arriving in front house. Husband back work. Husband say Honey I home, then little childrens running to him, see if he bringing gift.

But that not my life. That nothing to do with my life. I not having life in West. I not having home in West. I scared.

I no speaking English.

I fearing future.

'I no speaking English. I fearing future'

February

alien

alien adj foreign; repugnant (to); from another world
n foreigner; being from another world

Is UNBELIEVABLE, I arriving London, 'Heathlow Airport'.
Every single name very difficult remembering, because
just not 'London Airport' simple way like we simple way
call 'Beijing Airport'. Everything very confuse way here,
passengers is separating in two queues.

Sign in front of queue say: ALIEN and NON ALIEN.

I am alien, like Hollywood film *Alien*, I live in another
planet, with funny looking and strange language.

I standing in most longly and slowly queue with all
aliens waiting for visa checking. I feel little criminal but I
doing nothing wrong so far. My English so bad. How to do?

In my text book I study back China, it says English
peoples talk like this:

'How are you?'

'*I am very well. How are you?*'

'*I am very well.*'

Question and answer exactly the same!

Old saying in China: '*Birds have their bird language, beasts have their beast talk*' (鸟有鸟语,兽有兽言). English they totally another species.

Immigration officer holding my passport behind his accounter, my heart hanging on high sky. Finally he stamping on my visa. My heart touching down like air plane. Ah. Wo. Ho. Ha. Picking up my luggage, now I a legal foreigner. Because legal foreigner from Communism region, I must re-educate, must match this capitalism freedom and Western democracy.

All I know is: I not understanding what people say to me at all. From now on, I go with *Concise Chinese–English Dictionary* at all times. It is red cover, look just like *Little Red Book*. I carrying important book, even go to the toilet, in case I not knowing the words for some advanced machine and need checking out in dictionary. Dictionary is most important thing from China. *Concise* meaning simple and clean.

hostel

hostel n building providing accommodation at a low cost for a specific group of people such as students, travellers, homeless people, etc

FIRST NIGHT IN 'hostel'. Little *Concise Chinese–English Dictionary* hostel explaining: a place for 'people such as students, travellers and homeless people' to stay. Sometimes my dictionary absolute right. I am student and I am homeless looking for place to stay. How they knowing my situation *precisely*?

Thousands of additional words and phrases reflect scientific and technological innovations, as well as changes in politics, culture, and society. In particular, many new words and expressions as well as new usages and meanings which have entered the Chinese language as a result of China's open-door policy over the last decade have been included in the Chinese–English section of the dictionary.

That is sentence in *Preface*. All sentence in preface long like this, very in-understandable. But I must learning this stylish English because it high-standard English from authority. Is parents' command on me: studying how speak and write English in England, then coming back China, leaving job in government work unit and making lots money for their shoes factory by big international business relations. Parents belief their life is dog's life, but with money they save from last several years, I make better life through Western education.

Anyway, *hostel* called 'Nuttington House' in Brown Street, nearby Edward Road and Baker Street. I write all the names careful in notebook. No lost. Brown Street seem really brown with brick buildings everywhere. Prison look-ing. Sixteen pounds for per bed per day. With sixteen pounds, I live in top hotel in China with private bathroom. Now I must learn counting the money and being mean to myself and others. Gosh.

First night in England is headache.

Pulling large man-made-in-China-suitcase into *hostel*, second wheel fall off by time I open the door. (First wheel already fall off when I get suitcase from airport's luggage bell.) Is typical suitcase produced by any factory in Wen Zhou, my hometown. My hometown China's biggest home-products industry town, our government says. Coat hangers, plastic washbasins, clothes, leather belts and nearly-leather bags, computer components etc, we make there. Every family in my town is factory. Big factories export their products to everywhere in the world, just like my parents get order from Japan, Singapore and Israel. But anyway, one over-the-sea trip and I lost all the wheels. I swear I never buy any products made from home town again.

Standing middle of the room, I feeling strange. This is *The West*. By window, there hanging old red curtain with holes. Under feet, old blood-red carpet has suspicions dirty spots. Beddings, they covering by old red blanket too. Everything is dirty blood red.

Room smelling old, rotten. Suddenly my body feeling old too. 'English people respect history, not like us,' teachers say to us in schools. Is true. In China now, all buildings is no more than 10 years old and they already old enough to be demolished.

With my enormous curiosity, walking down to the night street. First night I away home in my entirely twenty-three years life, everything scare me. Is cold, late winter. Windy and chilli. I feeling I can die for all kinds of situation in every second. No safety in this country, I think unsafe feeling come from I knowing nothing about this country. I scared I in a big danger.

I scared by cars because they seems coming from any possible directing. I scared by long hair black man passing

because I think he beating me up just like in films. I scared
by a dog. Actually chained with old lady but I thinking dog
maybe have mad-dog-illness and it suddenly bite me and
then I in hospital then I have no money to pay and then I
sent back to China.

Walking around like a ghost, I see two rough mans in
corner suspicionly smoke and exchange something.
Ill-legal, I have to run – maybe they desperate drug addic-
tors robbing my money. Even when I see a beggar sleeping
in a sleep bag I am scared. Eyes wide open in darkness
staring at me like angry cat. What he doing here? I am
taught everybody in West has social security and medical
insurance, so, why he needs begging?

I going back quickly to Nuttington House. Red old carpet, red old curtain, red old blanket. Better switch off light.

Night long and lonely, staying nervously in tacky room.
London should be like emperor's city. But I cannot feel it.
Noise coming from other room. Laughing in drunkenly
way. Upstairs TV news speaking intensely nonsense.
Often the man shouting like mad in the street. I worry. I
worry I getting lost and nobody in China can find me
anymore. How I finding important places including Buckingham Palace, or Big Stupid Clock? I looking everywhere
but not seeing big posters of David Beckham, Spicy Girls
or President Margaret Thatcher. In China we hanging
them everywhere. English person not respect their heroes
or what?

No sleeping. Switching on the light again. Everything

turning red. Bloody new world. I study little red dictionary. English words made only from twenty-six characters?
Are English a bit lazy or what? We have fifty thousand
characters in Chinese.

Starting at page one:

A

Abacus: (meaning a wooden machine used
               for counting)

Abandon: (meaning to leave or throw away)

Abashed: (meaning to feel embrassed or
               regretful)

Abattoir: (meaning a place to kill the animals)

Abbess: (meaning the boss of woman monk's
               house)

Abbey: (meaning a temple)

Abbot: (meaning the boss of a temple)

Abbreviate: (meaning to write a word quickly)

Abduct: (meaning to tie somebody up and
               take away to somewhere)

Words becoming blurred and no meaning. The first night I
falling into darkness with the jet-lag tiredness.

full english breakfast

1. Builder's Super Platter:
double egg, beans, bacon, sausage, bubble,
mushroom, tomato, 2 toast, tea or coffee included.

2. Vegetarian Breakfast:
double egg, bubble, mushroom, beans, veggie
sausage, hash browns, tea or coffee included.

'TALK DOESN'T COOK *rice*,' say Chinese. Only thing I care in life is eating. And I learning English by food first, of course. Is most practical way.

Getting up early, I have free *Full English Breakfast* from my *hostel*. English so proud they not just say *hotel*, they say *Bed and Breakfast*, because breakfast so importantly to English situation. Even say 'B and B' everyone know what thinking about. Breakfast more important than Bed.

I never seeing a *breakfast* like that. Is big lunch for construction worker! I not believe every morning, my *hostel* offering everybody this meal, lasting three hours, from 7 clock to 10 clock. Food like messy scrumpled eggs, very salty bacons, burned bread, very thick milk, sweet bean in orange sauce, coffee, tea, milk, juice. Church or temple should be like this, giving the generosity to normal people. But 8.30 in the morning I refuse accepting two oily sausage, whatever it made by pork or by vegetables, is just too fat for a little Chinese.

What is this 'baked beans'? White colour beans, in orange sticky sweet sauce. I see some baked bean tins in shop when I arrive to London yesterday. Tin food is very expensive to China. Also we not knowing how to open it. So I never ever try tin food. Here, right in front of me, this baked beans must be very expensive. Delicacy is baked beans. Only problem is, tastes like somebody put beans into mouth but spit out and back into plate.

Sitting on breakfast table, my belly is never so full. Still two pieces of bread and several 'baked tomatoes' on my plate. I can't chew more. Feeling guilty and wasty, I take out little *Concise Chinese–English Dictionary* from my pocket, start study English. My language school not starting yet, so I have to learn by myself first. Old Chinese saying: 'the stupid bird should fly first before other birds start to fly' (笨鸟先飞).

When I am studying the word *Accommodate*, woman come clean table, and tell me I must leave. She must hate me that I eat too much food here. But not my fault.

First morning, I steal white coffee cup from table.

Second morning, I steal glass. So now in my room I can having tea or water. After breakfast I steal breads and boiled eggs for lunch, so I don't spending extra money on food. I even saving bacons for supper. So I saving bit money from my parents and using for cinema or buying books.

Ill-legal. I know. Only in this country three days and I already become thief. I never steal piece of paper in own country. Now I studying hard on English, soon I stealing their language too.

Nobody know my name here. Even they read the spelling of my name: *Zhuang Xiao Qiao*, they have no idea how saying it. When they see my name starts from 'Z', stop trying. I unpronouncable Ms Z.

First three days in this country, wherever I walk, the voice from my parents echo my ears:

'No talking strangers.'

'No talking where you live.'

'No talking how much money you have.'

'And most important thing: no trusting anybody.'

That my past life. Life before in China. The warns speaking in my mother's harsh local dialect, of course, translation into English by *Concise Chinese–English Dictionary*.

properly

proper adj real or genuine; suited to a particular purpose; correct in behaviour; excessively moral

TODAY MY FIRST time taking taxi. How I find important place with bus and tube? Is impossibility. Tube map is like plate of noodles. Bus route is in-understandable. In my home town everyone take cheap taxi, but in London is very expensive and taxi is like the Loyal family look down to me.

Driver say: 'Please shut the door properly!'

I already shut the door, but taxi don't moving.

Driver shout me again: 'Shut the door properly!' in a *concisely* manner.

I am bit scared. I not understanding what is this 'properly'.

'I beg your pardon?' I ask. 'What is *properly*?'

'Shut the door properly!' Taxi driver turns around his big head and neck nearly break because of anger.

'Tube map is like plate of noodles'

'But what is "properly", Sir?' I so frightened that I not daring ask it once more again.

Driver coming out from taxi, and walking to door. I think he going kill me.

He opens door again, smashing it back to me hardly.

'Properly!' he shout.

Later, I go in bookshop and check 'properly' in *Collins English Dictionary* ('THE AUTHORITY ON CURRENT ENGLISH'). *Properly* means 'correct behaviour'. I think of my behaviour with the taxi driver ten minutes ago. Why incorrect? I go to accounter buy little *Collins* for my pocket.

My small *Concise Chinese–English Dictionary* not having 'properly' meaning. In China we never think of 'correct behaviour' because every behaviour correct.

I want write these newly learned words everyday, make my own dictionary. So I learn English fast. I write down here and now, in every second and every minute when I hear a new noise from an English's mouth.

fog

fog n mass of condensed water vapour in the lower air, often greatly reducing visibility

'LONDON IS THE Capital of fog.' It saying in middle school textbook. We studying chapter from Charles Dickens's novel *Foggy City Orphan*. Everybody know Oliver Twist living in city with bad fog. Is very popular novel in China.

As soon as I arriving London, I look around the sky but no any fogs. 'Excuse me, where I seeing the fogs?' I ask policeman in street.

'Sorry?' he says.

'I waiting two days already, but no fogs,' I say.

He just look at me, he must no understanding of my English.

When I return Nuttington House from my tourism visiting, reception lady tell me: 'Very cold today, isn't it?' But why she tell me? I know this information, and now is too late, because I finish my tourism visiting, and I wet and freezing.

Today I reading not allowed to stay more than one week in hostel. I not understanding hostel's policy. 'Money can buy everything in capitalism country' we told in China. My parents always saying if you have money you can make the devil push your grind stone.

But here you not staying even if you pay. My parents wrong.

I checking all cheap flats on LOOT in Zone 1 and 2 of London and ringing agents. All agents sound like from Arabic countries and all called Ali. Their English no good too. One Ali charges Marble Arch area; one Ali charges Baker Street area. But I meet different Alis at Oxford Circus tube station, and see those houses. I dare not to move in. Places dirty and dim and smelly. How I live there?

London, by appearance, so noble, respectable, but when I follow these Alis, I find London a refuge camp.

beginner

beginner n person who has just started learning to do
something

HOLBORN. FIRST DAY studying my language school. Very
very frustrating.

'My name is Margaret Wilkinson, but please call me
Margaret,' my grammar teach tells in front blackboard. But
I must give respect, not just call Margaret. I will call Mrs
Margaret.

'What is grammar? Grammar is the study of the
mechanics and dynamics of language,' Mrs Margaret says
in the classroom.

I not understanding what she saying. Mrs Margaret
have a neatly cut pale blonde hair, with very serious
clothes. Top and her bottom always same colour. She not
telling her age, but I guessing she from 31 to 56. She

wearing womans style shoes, high heel black leather, very possible her shoes are all made in home town Wen Zhou, by my parents. She should know it, one day I tell her. So she not so proud in front of us.

Chinese, we not having grammar. We saying things simple way. No verb-change usage, no tense differences, no gender changes. We bosses of our language. But, English language is boss of English user.

Mrs Margaret teaching us about nouns. I discovering English is very scientific. She saying *nouns* have two types – countable and uncountable.

'You can say *a car*, but not *a rice*,' she says. But to me, *cars* are really uncountable in the street, and we can count the *rice* if we pay great attention to a rice bowl.

Mrs Margaret also explaining nouns is plural and singular.

'Jeans are pairs,' she says. But, everybody know jeans or trousers always one thing, you can't wear many jean or plural trouser. Four years old baby know that. Why waste ink adding 's'? She also saying nouns is three different gender: masculine, feminine, and neuter.

'A table is neuter,' she says.

But, who cares a table is neuter? Everything English so scientific and problematic. Unlucky for me because my science always very bad in school, and I never understanding mathematics. First day, already know I am *loser*.

After lunch breaking, Mrs Margaret introducing us little

about verbs. Gosh, verb is just crazy. Verb has verbs, verb-ed and verb-ing. And verbs has three types of mood too: indicative, imperative, subjunctive. Why so moody? 'Don't be too frustrated. You will all soon be speaking the Queen's English.' Mrs Margaret smiles to me.

pronoun

pronoun n word, such as she or it, used to replace a noun

FIRST WEEK IN language school, I speaking like this:

'Who is her name?'

'It costing I three pounds buying this disgusting sandwich.'

'Sally telling I that her just having coffee.'

'Me having fried rice today.'

'Me watching TV when me in China.'

'Our should do things together with the people.'

Always the same, the people laughing as long as I open my mouth.

'Ms Zh-u-ang, you have to learn when to use *I* as the subject, and when to use *me* as the object!'

Mrs Margaret speaking Queen's English to me.

So *I* have two *mes*? According to Mrs Margaret, one is

subject *I* one is object *I*? But I only one I. Unless Mrs Margaret talking about incarnation or after life.

She also telling me I disorder when speaking English. Chinese we starting sentence from concept of *time* or *place*. Order like this:

Last autumn on the Great Wall we eat barbecue.

So time and space always bigger than little human in our country. Is not like order in English sentence, 'I', or 'Jake' or 'Mary' by front of everything, supposing be most important thing to whole sentence.

English a sexist language. In Chinese no 'gender definition' in sentence. For example, Mrs Margaret says these in class:

'Everyone must do *his* best.'

'If a pupil can't attend the class, he should let *his* teacher know.'

'We need to vote for a *chairman* for the student union.'

Always talking about mans, no womans!

Mrs Margaret later telling verb most difficult thing for our oriental people. Is not only 'difficult', is 'impossibility'! I not understanding why verb can always changing.

One day I find a poetry by William Shakespeare on school's library shelf. I studying hard. I even not stopping for lunch. I open little *Concise Dictionary* more 40 times checking new words. After looking some Shakespeare poetry, I will can return back my China home, teaching everyone about Shakespeare. Even my father know Shakespeare big dude, because our in our local government evening classes they telling everyones Shakespeare most famous person from Britain.

One thing, even Shakespeare write bad English. For example, he says 'Where go thou?'. If I speak like that Mrs Margaret will tell me wrongly. Also I finding poem of him call 'An Outcry Upon Opportunity':

> 'Tis thou that execut'st the traitor's treason;
> Thou sett'st the wolf where he the lamb may get

I not understanding at all. What this ''tis', 'execut'st' and 'sett'st'? Shakespeare can writing that, my spelling not too bad then.

After grammar class, I sit on bus and have deep thought about my new language. Person as dominate subject, is main thing in an English sentence. Does it mean West culture respecting individuals more? In China, you open daily newspaper, title on top is 'OUR HISTORY DECIDE IT IS TIME TO GET RICH' or 'THE GREAT COMMUNIST PARTY HAVE THIRD MEETING' or 'THE 2008 OLYMPICS NEED CITIZENS PLANT MORE GREENS'. Look, no subjects here are mans or womans. Maybe Chinese too shaming putting their name first, because that not modest way to be.

slogan

slogan n catchword or phrase used in politics or advertising

I GO IN bookshop buy the English version of *Little Red Book*. Not easy read but very useful argue with English using Chairman Mao *slogans*. English version is without translator name on cover. Yes, no second name can be shared on Mao's work. Chairman Mao

> has inherited, defended and developed Marxism-Leninism with genius, creatively and comprehensively and has brought it to a higher and completely new stage.

The English translators of this book, they are like feather compare with Tai Mountain.

In West, Mao's words work for me, though they not

work in China now. Example, today big confusion in streets. Everywhere people marching to say no to war in Iraq.

'No war for oil!'

'Listen to your people!'

The demon-strators from everywhere in Britain, social-ists, Communists, teachers, students, housewifes, labour workers, Muslim womans covered under the scarf with their children . . . They marching to the Hyde park. I am in march because I not finding way to hostel. So no choice except following. I search Chinese faces in the march team. Very few. Maybe they busy and desperately earning money in those Chinese Takeaways.

People in march seems really happy. Many smiles. They feel happy in sunshine. Like having weekend family picnic. When finish everyone rush drink beers in pubs and ladies gather in tea houses, rub their sore foots.

Can this kind of demon-stration stop war?

From Mao's little red book, I learning in school:

A revolution is not a dinner party, or writing an essay, or painting a picture, or doing embroidery; it cannot be so refined, so leisurely and gentle, so temperate, kind, courteous, restrained and mag-nanimous. A revolution is an insurrection, an act of violence with which one class overthrows another.

Probably Communist love war more than anybody. From Mao's opinion, war able be 'Just' although it is bloody. (But blood happen everyday anyway . . .) He say:

Oppose unjust war with just war, whenever possible.

So if people here want to against war in Iraq, they needing have civil war with their Tony Blair here, or their Bush. If more people bleeding in native country, then those mens not making war in other place.

weather

weather n day-to-day atmospheric conditions of a place
v (cause to) be affected by the weather; come safely through

weather n the state of the atmosphere at a place and time
in terms of temperature, wind, rain, etc

CARRYING MEAT BALL and pork slice from supermarket,
now I am in place calling *Ye Olde English Tea Shop*. What is
this 'Ye'? Why 'Olde' not 'Old'? Wrong spelling.

Tea house like Qing dynasty old style building waiting
for being demolish. Everything looking really old here,
especial wood stick beam in middle of house, supporting
roof. Old carpet under the foot is very complication flower
pattern, like something from emperor mother house.

'Where would you like to sit?', 'What can I get you?', 'A
table for one person?', 'Are you alone?' Smiling waiter ask
so many questions. He making me feel bit lonely. In China

I not have loneliness concept. Always we with family or crowd. But England, always alone, and even waiter always remind you you are alone . . .

Everybody listening the weather at this moment in tea house. All time in London, I hearing weather report from radios. It tells weather situation like emergency typhoon coming. But no emergency coming here. I checking *Concise Chinese–English Dictionary*. It saying all English *under the weather*, and all English is *weather beaten*, means uncomfortable. Is reasonable, of course. England everybody beaten by the weather. Always doubt or choice about weather. Weather it rain or weather it sunshine, you just not know.

Weather report also very difficult understand. The weather man not saying 'rain' or 'sunny' because they speaking in complication and big drama way. He reporting weather like reporting big war: 'Unfortunately . . . Hopefully . . .'. I listen two hours radio I meet twice weather report. Do they think British Empire as big China that it need to report at any time? Or clouds in this country changing every single minute? Yes, look at the clouds now, they are so suspicious! Not like my home town, often several weeks without one piece cloud in sky and weather man has nothing more to say. Some days he just saying 'It is Yin', which mean weather is negative.

confusion

confuse v mix up; perplex, disconcert; make unclear

ENGLISH FOOD VERY confusing. They eating and drinking strange things. I think even Confucius have great confusion if he studying English.

It is already afternoon about 3 o'clock and I so hungry. What can I eat, I asking waiter. He offering 'Afternoon Tea'. What? Eat afternoon tea?

So he showing me blackboard, where is a menu:

Whatever, I must to eat whatever they have or I faint. Three minutes later my thing arrives: 'scones' hot and thick and dry, cream is unbelieveable, butter is greasy, and jam are three kinds: raspberry, cramberry and strawberry. A white tea pot with a white tea cup.

I confusing again when I look at 'whipped cream' on little blackboard. What is that mean? How people whip the cream? I see a poster somewhere near Chinatown. On poster naked woman only wears leather boots and leather pants, and she whipping naked man kneeling down under legs. So a English chef also whipping in kitchen?

I put scones into mouth, and drink tea like horse. Next door me, I hearing somebody wanting 'frothy coffee'.

A lady with a young man. She say: 'Can I have a frothy coffee, please? And my friend will have a black coffee, with skimmed milk.'

It must be big work making something 'skimmed', and 'frothy', and 'whipped'. Why drinking become so complicating and need so much work?

And water are even more complicating here. Maybe raining everyday here and too much water so English making lots kind water.

I thirsty from eating dry scones.

Waiter asks me: 'What would you like? Still water, or filthy water?'

'What? Filthy water?' I am shocked.

'OK, filthy water.' He leave and fetch bottle of water.

I so curious about strange water. I opening bottle, immediately lots bubbles coming out. How they putting bubbles in water? Must be highly technicaled. I drinking it. Taste bitter, very filthy, not natural at all, like poison.

homesick

homesick adj sad because missing one's home and family

IN MY LANGUAGE school, Mrs Margaret ask me:

'Would you like some tea?'

'No,' I say.

She looking at me, her face suddenly frozen. Then she asking me again:

'Would you like some coffee then?'

'No. I don't want.'

'Are you sure you don't want anything?'

'No. I don't want anything wet,' I saying loudly, precisely.

Mrs Margaret looking very upset.

But why she asking me again and again? I already answer her from first time.

'Oh, dear.' Mrs Margaret sigh heavy. Then she standing up, and starting make her own tea. She drink it in very thirsty way, like angry camel in the desert. I am confusing. Am I make tea for her before she asking me? But how do I know she thirsty if she not telling me directly? All this *manners* very complication. China not have *politeness* in same way.

And how to learn be *polite* if I not getting chance talk people? I am always alone, talking in my notebook, or wandering here and there like invisible ghost. Nobody speak to me and I not dare open my mouth first because when I start talking, I asking the rude questions.

'Excuse me, you know there are some red spots on your face?'

'Are you a bit fatter than me?'

'I don't believe we same age. You look much older than me.'

'I think you are a very normal person. Not a special person.'

'The food you cook is disgusting. Why nobody tell you?'

I already have very famous reputation in my language school. They say: 'You know that Chinese girl . . .' 'Which one?' 'That rude one of course!' I hear it several times. Maybe I need get trained from 'Manners International Etiquette Workshop', which is advertisement I read on Chinese newspaper. It say:

Manners International custom tailors each etiquette program to the specific requirements of each individual, business/corporation, organization, school, Girl Scout Troop, or family.

I think I am exactly that 'individual' needing to be taught there, if fee is not too expensive. Re-education is always important.

Mrs Margaret look at me in sad way. 'You must be very *homesick*,' she says.

Actually not missing family at all, and not missing boring little hometown also. I happy I not needing think about stinking shoes with anyhow the same style on showroom shelfs in parent factory. I glad I not having go work every day at work unit. Only thing I missing is food. Roasted ducks, fresh cut lamb meat in boiling hot pot, and red chilli spicy fish . . . When thinking of food, I feel I make big mistake by leaving China.

This country to me, this a new world. I not having past in this country. No memory being builded here so far, no sadness or happiness so far, only information, hundreds and thousands of information, which confuse me everyday.

Except my English class every morning, I so bored of being alone. I always alone, and talking to myself. When sky become dark, I want grab something warm in this cold country. I want find friend teach me about this strange country. Maybe I want find man can love me. A man in this country save me, take me, adopt me, be my family, be my home. Every night, when I write diary, I feeling troubled. Am I writing in Chinese or in English? I trying express me, but confusing – I see other little me try expressing me in other language.

Maybe I not need feeling lonely, because I always can talk to other 'me'. Is like seeing my two pieces of lips speaking in two languages at same time. Yes, I not lonely, because I with another me. Like Austin Power with his Mini Me.

'I trying express me, but confusing – I see other little me try expressing me in other language'

progressive tenses

(Also called 'Continuous Tenses') Progressive tenses are made with TO BE + – ING. The mose common use of the progressive form is to talk about an action or situation that is already going on at a particular moment we are thinking about. But the 'going to' structure and the present progressive can also be used to talk about the future.

PEOPLE SAY 'I'M going to go to the cinema . . .'

Why there two *go* for one sentence? Why not enough to say one *go* to go?

> *I am going to go to the supermarket to buy some porks?*
> *You are going to go to the Oxford circus to buy clothes?*
> *He is going to go to the park for a walk?*

'I go' is enough to expressing 'I am going to go . . .' Really.

———

This afternoon, I am going to go to cinema watch double bill – *Breakfast at Tiffiny's* and *Some Like it Hot*. Double bill, they letting people pay one time but twice of the bill, how clever the business here! Cinema is my paradise. When a person not having any idea about real life, just walk into cinema choosing a film to see. In China, I seeing some American films, like *Titanic*, and *Rush Hours*, but of course Hollywood stars speaking Mandarin to us, and I can sing soundtrack from *Titanic*, 'My heart goes on and on', only in Chinese translation.

American films strange in London. People at Language School tell me use student card, I can have cheap cinema ticket. Last week I go Prince Charles in Chinatown. They say is cheapest cinema in London. Two films screening: *Moholland Driver*, and *Blue Velvet*. All together is more than 4 hours. Perfect for my lonely night. So I buy tickets and get in.

Gosh what crazy films. I not understanding very much the English speakings, but I understand I must never walk in highway at night alone. The world scary and strange like deep dark dream. Leaving cinema, trembling, I try find bus to home, but some mean kids teasing at each other on bus stop. Shouting and swearing bit like terrorist. Old man drunk in street and walk to me saying words I not understanding. Maybe he think I prostitute. England is hopeless country, but people having everything here: Queen, Buckingham Place, Loyal Family, oldest and slowest tube, BBC, Channel 4, W. H. Smith, Marx & Spencer, Tesco, Soho, millennium bridge, Tate Modern, Oxford Circus, London Tower, Cider and ale, even Chinatown.

Anyway, after *Breakfast at Tiffany* where posh woman dressing like prostitute and *Some Like It Hot* where mans dressing like womans, I go back my new home which have cheap renting 65 pounds per week. It is ugly place. It smelling pee in every corner of street. Nearby tube station called Tottenham Hale.

House is two floors, lived by Cantonese family: housewife, husband who work as chef in Chinatown, and 16-year-old British-accent son. Is like one child policy still carried on here. The garden is concrete, no any green things. Very often little wild grass growing and come out between the concretes, but housewife pull and kill grass immediately. She is grass killer. The lush next doors trees trying come through rusty iron fence, but nothing getting in this concrete family. This house like factory place in China, just for cheap labours earning money, no life, no green, and no love.

Family speaks Cantonese so I not understanding them. Chinese moon calendar is on wall. Wok, chopsticks, Mah Jong, Chinese cable TV programmes . . . everything inside house is traditional. Not much fun. Outside, view is rough. Old rusty railway leading to maybe more interesting place. Walking along railway I see nearby shopping centre, a McDonalds, a KFC, a Burger King, a petrol station called 'Shell', a sad looking Tottenham Hale tube station.

Every night I coming out Tottenham Hale tube station and walking home shivering. I scared to pass each single dark corner. In this place, crazy mans or sporty kids throwing stones to you or shouting to you without reasons. Also, the robbers robbing the peoples even poorer than them. In China we believe 'rob the rich to feed the poor'. But robbers here have no poetry.

'Dare to struggle and dare to win.' Chairman Mao's words like long time no see friend coming to me. I need somebody protect me, accompany me, but not staring at me in darkness. I longing for smile from man, longing for smile even only remaining several seconds.

March

homosexual

homosexual adj (person) sexually attracted to members of the same sex

I MEET YOU in the cinema. It is film called *Fear Eats Soul*, from German director Rainer Werner Fassbinder. Programme say Fassbinder is *homosexual*. What is it? Now I have this *Collins English Dictionary* – THE AUTHORITY ON CURRENT ENGLISH. It tells me what is *Homosexual*. Strange word, I cannot imagine it.

It is the Ciné-Lumière, near South Kensington. 7 o'clock Monday, raining. Not over ten people, half are old couple with white hair. Then there you are.

You are alone. You sit almost beside me. Two seats between us. Your face quite pale in the dim light, but beautiful. I too am alone in the cinema. I always alone in the cinema before I meet you. I am bit confused whether if cinema make me less lonely or even more lonely.

On the screen, old German woman dancing with young black man in a pub. All the peoples in pub watching. Old woman she has humble smile. She has hard life. Then I see your smile in the dark light. Why I can see your smile while I am watching the film? You turn your face and understand I am looking at you. You smile again, but very gentle, and very little. You look back the screen.

You have warm smile. Is like a baby's smile. Nobody smile to me before like you in this cold country. In the darkness, I am thinking you must be kind man.

It is a film shows impossible love between old white woman and young black man. But nothing to do with 'homosexual'.

After film, we walk to exit. Our bodies so close. Out from cinema, road lights finally light up our faces.

Then, with gentle smile, you ask me:

'Did you like the film?'

I nod head.

Is like the uncomfortable English weather have some sunshine suddenly.

You ask my name. I say name start from Z, 'But please no worry to remember,' I say, 'my name too long pronounce.' You tell me your name, but how I remember English name? Western name are un-rememberable, like all Western look the same. But I want remember you, want remember the difference you with others. I look at your face. Brown eyes, transparent. Thick brown hair, like colour of leafs in autumn. Your voice gentle, but solid. It sound safe.

We walk from South Kensington towards Hyde Park. A long way for feets. What we talk about? I tell you of famous English creamy tea. You say prefer French Patisserie.

'Patty surly?'

'No *patisserie*.'

'How spell?'

'P-a-t-i-s-s-e-r-i-e.' You speak slowly with slowly moving lips, like Mrs Margaret.

'What is it?' I not bring dictionary tonight.

You stop in front very fashionable 'French Patisserie' shop. Still open at late time. Beautiful cakes waiting inside window.

'Which one would you like?' You look at me.

I worried of price.

'I don't know,' I say. How I know about these soft stuffs?

'Then I'll choose one for you.'

You give me a piece of creamy thing.

'What is it?' I hold it on my hand carefully.

'c-h-o-c-o-l-a-t-e e-c-l-a-i-r.'

'OK.'

I bite it, but immediately cream squeeze out, falling on street.

I look at white cream drop on dirty street.

You look at white cream drop on dirty street.

'Oh well, never mind,' you say.

So we talk, and talk, and talk, through Hyde Park, then to West End, then Islington, walk towards my place. Nearly four hours walking. My legs is so sore, and my throat so dry, but I enjoying it. Is first time a person walking beside me through chilly night. Is also first time a person being patience listen my nonsense English, and learning me bad language. You much better than Mrs Margaret. She never let us talk freely.

When I arriving back, is already deep night.

In front of house, you kiss my two cheeks, and watch me go in door.

'Good meeting you,' you say.

Everything happen in very gentle way.

I want go immediately my room think about English man who smile and kiss me like lover, but I see Chinese landlord sitting on kitchen, watching TV and waiting for me. He is yawning. He worried my late back. At same time wife come down from upstairs bedroom in sleeping robe:

'We were so worried about you! We never come back as late as you do!'

Nervous voice remind me of my mother. My mother always talk to me like that.

I say I OK. Don't worry.

Wife look at me seriously: 'It is dangerous at night and also you are a young girl.'

I take off my guilty shoes.

'Next time if you are late, phone my husband and he can come and pick you up. This is England not China. Men easily get drunk in the pub!'

With last yawn, husband turn off TV. He look cross and tired.

I feel good after I close my bedroom's door. My heart hold a secret to make me warm at night.

The leafs blow outside. The street lights shine on my window. I am thinking I am only person to be awake in the world. I am thinking of China, thinking of old German lady dancing, thinking of your smile. I fall to sleep with sweet feelings inside my body.

guest

guest n person entertained at another's house or at another's expense; invited performer or speaker; customer at a hotel or restaurant

A NEW DAY. You call me. At once I know your voice. You ask if I want visit Kew Gardens.

'Queue Gardens?'

'Meet me at Richmond tube station,' you say. 'R-i-c-h-m-o-n-d.'

Is beautiful weather. What a surprise. And so peaceful in the grassy space. So green. Cherry blossoms is just coming out and you tell me about your favourite snowdrops. We see there is different small gardens with different theme. Africa garden are palm trees. North America garden are rocks. South America garden are cactus. And there is too Asia gardens. I so happy Manager not forgetting Asia gardens.

But I so disappointing after we walk in. Lotuses and bamboos is growing in India garden, plum trees and stone bridge is growing in Japanese garden. Where is my Chinese garden?

'Doesn't look like they've made a Chinese garden,' you say to me.

'But that very unfair,' I say in angry voice. 'Bamboos belongs to China. Panda eats bamboos leafs in China, you must hear, no?'

You laugh. You say you agree. They should move some plants from India and Japan garden to make Chinese garden.

The meadow asking us to lie. We rest beside each other. I never do that with a man. Juice from grass wetting my white shirt. My heart melting. Sky is blue and airplane flying above us, low and clear. I see moving shadows of the plane on the meadow.

'I want see where you live,' I say.

You look in my eyes. 'Be my guest.'

misunderstanding

misunderstand v fail to understand properly

THAT'S HOW ALL start. From a misunderstanding. When you say 'guest' I think you meaning I can stay in your house. A week later, I move out from Chinese landlord.

I not really have anything, only big wheel-missing suitcase. The husband helping me suitcase. The wife opening door. Your white van waiting outside, you with hands on wheel.

Husband puts wheel-missing suitcase on your van, you smile to landlord and turn engine key.

I want ask something to my landlord that I always wanting ask, so I put my head out of window:

'Why you not plant plants in your garden?'

Wife is hesitate: 'Why? It is not easy to grow plants in this country. No sun.'

For last time I look the concrete garden. Is same no

story, same way as before. Like little piece of Gobi desert. What a life! Or maybe all the immigrants here living like that?

White van starting up, I respond to wife:

'Not true. Everywhere green in this country. How you say not easy growing plant here?'

We leave house behind. The couple is waving hands to me.

I say: 'Chinese strange sometimes.'

You smile: 'I don't understand you Chinese at all. But I would like to get to know you.'

We driving in high street. My suitcase lie down obediently at back. Is so easy move house like this in West? I happy I leave my grey and no fun Tottenham Hale, heading to a better area, I think. But streets becoming more and more rough. Lots of black kids shouting outside. Beggars sitting on corner with dogs, smoking, and murmuring.

'Where your house?' I ask.

'Hackney.'

'How is Hackney?'

'Hackney is Hackney,' you say.

bachelor

bachelor n unmarried man; person who holds the lowest university or college degree

YOUR HOUSE IS old house standing lonely between ugly new buildings for poor people. Front, it lemon yellow painted. Both side of house is bricks covered by mosses and jasmine leafs. Through leafs I see house very damp and damaged. Must have lots of stories happened inside this house.

And you are really *bachelor*. Your bed is single bed. Made by several piece of big wood, with wooden boxes underneath. Old bedding sheets cover it. Must be very hard for sleep, like Chinese peasants *kang* bed. In kitchen, teacups is everywhere. Every cup different with other, big or small, half new or broken . . . So everything single, no company, no partner, no pair.

First day I arrive, our conversation like this:

I say: '*I eat. Do you eat?*'

You correct me in proper way: '*I want to eat. Would you like to eat something with me?*'

You ask: '*Would you like some coffee?*'

I say: '*I don't want coffee. I want tea.*'

You change it: '*A cup of tea would be delightful.*'

Then you laughing at my confusing face, and you change your saying: '*I would love a cup of tea, please.*'

I ask: 'How you use word "love" on tea?'

First time you make food for me it is some raw leafs with two boiled eggs. Eggy Salad. Is that all? Is that what English people offer in their homes? In China, cold food for *guest* is bad, only beggars no complain cold food. Maybe you don't know how cook, because you are a *bachelor*.

I sit down on your kitchen table, eat silently. Lampshade is on top of my head, tap is dripping in sink. So quiet. Scarily. I never ate such a quiet food in China. Always with many of family members, everybody shouting and screaming while eating. Here only the noise is from me using the forks and knife. I drop the knife two times so I decide only use one fork in my right hand.

Chewing. Chewing. No conversation.

You look at me eating, patiently.

Finally you ask: '*So, do you like the food?*'

I nod, put another leaf into my mouth. I remember me is bad speak with food full of my mouth. You wait. But patience maybe running out, so you answer your question in my voice: '*Yes, I like the food very much. It is delicious. It is yami.*'

The memory becomes so uncertain.

The memory keeps a portrait about you. An abstract portrait like pictures I saw in Tate Modern, blur details and sketchy lines. I start draw this picture, but my memory about you keep changing, and I have to change the picture.

green fingers

green fingers *Brit. informal* skill in gardening

OUR FIRST NIGHT. First time we make love. First time in my life doing this.

I think you are beautiful. You are beautiful smiles, and beautiful face, and beautiful language. You speak slowly. I almost hear every single word because you speak so slowly, only sometime I not understanding what you mean. But I understanding you more than anybody else I meet in England.

Then you are taking off clothes.

I look at you. Man's body seems ugly. Hair, bones, muscles, skins, more hair. I smell at you. Strong smell. Smell animal. Smell is from your hair, your chest, your neck, your armpit, your skin, your every single little bit in body.

Strong smell and strong soul. I even can feel it and

touch it. And I think your body maybe beautiful also. Is the home of your soul.

I ask how old are you, is first question Chinese people ask to stranger. You say forty-four. Older than me twenty years. Forty-four in my Chinese think is old, is really old. Leaves far behind away from youth. I say age sound old, but you look young. You say thanks, and you don't say more.

I say I think you beautiful, ignoring the age. I think you too beautiful for me, and I don't deserve of you.

Very early morning. You are sleeping, with gentle breathe. I look through bedroom's window. Sky turning dim into bright. I see small dried up old grapes hang under vines by window. Their shapes are become clear and clear in cold spring morning light. Garden is messy and lush. Your clothes and socks hanging in washing line. Your gardening machines everywhere on soil.

You are man, handy and physical. This is man's garden.

You make me feel fragile. Love makes me feel fragile, because I am not beautiful, I never being told I am beautiful. My mother always telling me I am ugly. 'You are ugly peasant girl. You have to know this.' Mother tells this to me for all twenty-three years. Maybe why I not never having boyfriend like other Chinese girls my age. When I badly communicating with others, my mother's words becomes loud in my eardrum. I am ugly peasant girl. I am ugly peasant girl.

'My body is crying for you,' you say.

Most beautiful sentence I heard in my life.

My bad English don't match your beautiful language.

I think I fall in love with you, but my love cannot match your beauty.

And then daytime. Sun puts light through garden to our bed. Birds are singing on roof. I think how sunlight must make people much happier in this dark country, and then I watch you wake up. We see each other naked, without distance. In light of reality. 'Good morning,' you say. 'You look even more lovely than yesterday.' And we make love again in the morning.

fertilise

fertilise v provide (an animal or plant) with sperm or pollen to bring about fertilisation; supply (soil) with nutrients

YOU TAKE ME to garden. Is very small, maybe ten square metres. One by one, you introduce me all the plants you have put there. Sixteen different plants in a ten square metres garden. In my home town in China, there only one plant in fields: rice.

You know every single plant's name, like they your family and you try tell me but I not remember English names so you write them down:

Potato	Green beans
Daffodil	Wisteria
Lavender	Grape vine
Mint	Bay tree
Spinach	Geranium

Thyme	Beetroot
Dill	Sweet corn
Apple tree	Fig tree

Then I tell you all these plants have very different names and meanings in Chinese. So I write down names in Chinese, and explain every word at you.

Potato   土豆
          earth bean

Daffodil 水仙
          fairy maiden from the water

Lavender 熏衣草
          clothes perfuming weeds

Mint   薄荷
          light lotus

Spinach   菠菜
          watery vegetable

Thyme   百里香
          one hundred miles fragrant

Dill   莳萝
          the herb of time

Apple tree 苹果树
          clover fern fruit tree

Green beans 豆子
          son of beans

Wisteria 紫藤
          purple vines

Grape vine	葡萄
	crawling plant
Bay tree	月桂树
	moon laurel
Geranium	天竺葵
	sky bamboo flower
Beetroot	甜菜
	sweet vegetable
Sweet corn	玉米
	jade rice
Fig tree	无花果树
	the fruit tree without flowers

You laughing when you hear the names. 'I never knew flutes grew on trees,' you say. It seems I am big comedy to you. I not understand why so funny. 'You can't say your Rs. It's *fruit* not *flute*,' you explain me. 'A *flute* is a musical instrument. But your Chinese name seems just right: a fig tree really is a fruit tree without flowers.'

'How a tree can just have fruit without having flower first?' I ask.

Like teacher, you describe how insect climbs into fruit to fertilise seed.

What 'fertilise'? I need looking in *Concise Chinese-English Dictionary*.

'Fertilise' make me think Chairman Mao. He likes fertiliser. Was big Mao thing increase productivity, increase plants. Maybe that why China, biggest peasants population country, still alive and become stronger after using fertiliser on the soil.

I ask: 'How long a fig tree has figs after insects fertilising it? Like woman have ten months pregnant?'

You look at me, like look at *alien*.

'Why ten months? I thought it took nine months,' you say.

'Chinese we say *shi yue huai tai* (十月怀胎). It means giving the birth after ten months pregnant.'

'That's strange.' You seem like want to laugh again. 'Which day do you start to count the pregnancy in China?' you ask seriously. But how I know? We never being taught this *properly* in school. Too shameful to teach and to study for our Chinese.

Standing under your fruit tree without flowers, I pick up piece of leaf, and put on my palm. A single leaf, but large. I touch the surface and feel hairy.

'Have you read the Bible?' you ask.

'No.' Of course not, not in China.

You fetch a big huge black book from room. You open the pages. 'Actually the fig tree is the oldest of mankind's symbols.' You point at beginning of book:

And the eyes of them both were opened, and they knew that they were naked, and they sewed fig leaves together, and made themselves aprons.

'What is that?' I am curious.

'It is about Adam and Eve. They used fig leaves to cover their naked bodies.'

'They clever. They knowing fig leaves bigger than other leafs,' I say.

You laugh again.

Your gardening machines everywhere in disorder.

Spade	铲子	
	For cutting the soil	
Fork	叉子	
	For soften the soil	
Rake	靶子	
	For scratching the grass	

Suddenly I bit shocked, stop. There are some nudity in your garden.

'What this?' I ask.

'Those are my sculptures,' you say.

Sculptures? A naked man no head, facing to ground of the garden. Body twisted, with enormous hands and enormous feet. Close to ground, between the legs, two beautiful eggs, like two half of apples. In the middle of apples, a penis like little wounded bird. I walk to him and touch. Is made of plaster. I amazed by this body, is huge, looks suffered. I remember picture from Michelangelo's *David* on your bookshelf, a very healthy and balanced body. But yours, yours far different.

Beside this body statue, some other smalls clay sculptures. Ear, big like basin, in brown. Shape of that ear spread like a big flower. Then more ears, different shape, different size. They lie on the grass quietly, listening us.

Under fig tree another penis made from clay, gentle, innocent. Then another one, looks harder, lies down beside honeysuckle roots, in soil colour. Little clay sculptures there, like they live with plants hundred years.

The noisy London being stopped by brick wall. The grey city kept away by this garden. Plants and sculptures on sunshine. Glamorous, like you. Maybe all mans in London green fingers. Maybe this country too cold and too dim, so plants and garden can showing imagination the spring, the sun, the warmth. And plants and garden giving love like womans warm mans life.

When I stand in garden with sixteen different plants, I think of Chinese mans. Chinese city-mans not plant-lover at all. Shameful for Chinese city-mans pour passion onto those leafs. He be considered a loser, no position in society. But you, you different. Who are you?

vegetarian

vegetarian n person who eats no meat or fish
adj suitable for a vegetarian

ONE PROBLEM BETWEEN us and that is food.

Chop Chop, local Chinese restaurant in Hackney. I make you go there even though you say you never go Chinese restaurants.

Restaurant has very plain looking. White plastic table and plastic chairs and white fluorescent lamp. Just like normal government work unit in China. Waiter unhappy when cleans table, not looking anybody. Woman with pony tails behind counter she even more mean. A plastic panda-savings-tin sitting on top of counter. None of them can speak Mandarin.

'No. Sit there. No, no, not this table. Sit at that table.'

Waiter commands like we is his soldiers.

'What you want? . . . We don't have tap water, you have

to order something from the menu . . . We don't do pots of green tea, only cups.'

I hate them. I swear I never been so rude Chinese restaurant in my entirely life. Why Chinese people becoming so mean in the West? I feel bit guilty for horrible service. Because I bring you, and you maybe thinking my culture just like this. Maybe that why some English look down of our Chinese. I am shameful for being a Chinese here.

But we still have to eat. Especially me, starving like the Ghost of Hunger. I always hungry. Even after big meal, later by one or two hours I feel hungry again. My family always very poor until several years ago. We used eat very small, barely had meat. After my parents started shoes factory, and left the poor peasants background behind, changed. But still I think foods all the time.

You not know nothing about Chinese food so I quickly order: duck, pork, fried tofu with beefs.

Meal comes to table, and I digging fastly my chopsticks into dishes like having a snowstorm. But you don't have any action at all. You just look me, like looking a Beijing opera.

'Why you not eat?' I ask, busy chewing my pork in my mouth.

'I am not very hungry,' you say.

'You use chopsticks?' I think maybe that's the reason.

'Yes. Don't worry.' You raise your chopsticks and perform to me.

'But you waste the food. Not like Chinese food?'

'I am a *vegetarian*,' you say picking up little bit rice. 'This menu is a zoo.'

I am surprised. I try find my dictionary. Damn, is not with me this time. I remember film *English Patient* I watch on pirate DVD in China to education me about British people. 'What that word? Word describe a people fall asleep for long long time, like living dying?'

'You mean coma?' You are confused.

'Yes, that is the word! You are not like that, do you?'

You put chopsticks down. Maybe you angry now.

'I presume you are thinking of the *persistent vegetative state*,' you say. '*Vegetarian* means you don't eat meat.'

'Oh, I am sorry,' I say, swallowing big mouthful tofus and beefs.

Now I understand why never buy piece of meat. I thought it is because you poor.

'Why don't eat meat? Meat very nutritious.'

'. . .' You have no comments.

'Also you be depression if you don't eating meat.'

'. . .' You still have no comments.

'My parents beaten me if I don't eating meat or any food on table in a meal. My parents curse me being picky and spoiled. Because others dying without any food to eat.'

'. . .' Still don't say anything.

'How come man is vegetarian? Unless he is monk,' I say.

Still no words from you, but laughing.

You watch me eating all of meal. I try finish the duck,

and the tofu and the beefs. My stomach painful. There are still porks left, and I order to take them away.

While I eating, you write top ten favourite food on a napkin:

lettuce

lentils

carrot

broccoli

radish

aubergine

avocado

pumpkin

spinach

asparagus

But, is this list will be the menu in our kitchen for rest of life? Is terrible! What about my meatball, my mutton, my beefs in black bean sauce? Who will be in charge of kitchen?

April

chinese cabbage + english slug

cabbage n vegetable with a large head of green leaves

slug n land snail with no shell; a bullet; a mouthful of an alcoholic

HARDLY DAYS IS absolutely sunny, sunny until sun falling to the west. Sky in England always look suspicious, untrustful, like today's. You see me sad but don't understand why.

Standing in the garden, you ask me: 'Do you want to have your own little plants in this garden? I think it should be a woman's garden as well.'

'Yes. I want. I want plant Chinese cabbages, some water lily, some plum tree, and maybe some bamboos, and maybe some Chinese chives as well . . .'

I immediately image picture of tradition Chinese garden.

'No, honey, it's too small for so many Chinese plants.'

Then, Sunday, we went to Columbia Road Flower Market. It my favourite market. We brought the small little sprouts of Chinese cabbage at home. Eight little sprouts all together.

We plant all these little things. Digging the soil, and putting every single sprout into the hole. You are fast than me. So you finished planting five, and I only putting third one in the little hole.

We watering Chinese cabbage sprouts every morning, loyal and faithful, like every morning we never forgetting brushing our teeth. Seeing tiny sprouts come out, my heart feel happy. Is our love. We plant it.

You say:

'Growing a vegetable and seeing it grow is more interesting than anything else. It's magic. Don't you agree?'

Yes. Is interesting. But in China, is just for peasant. Every person can do this, nothing special for growing food. Why so different here?

Then we see some little leafs come out but are bitten by the slug.

'It's dangerous that the slugs keep eating the small sprouts. They can die really easily,' you tell me.

Carrying with torch, every night, around 11 o'clock, you sneek into garden and check the slug. They are always several slug hidden behind the young leafs. Enjoying the delicious meal under the moonlight. You taking them out from the leafs, one by one. You putting these slug together in one glass bottle. Soon glass bottle becomes a slug-zoo.

'What your favourite words? Give me ten,' I say when we are sitting in garden. I want learn most beautiful English words because you are beautiful. I even not care whether if useful.

A piece of blank paper, a pen.

You writing it down, one by one.

'*Sea, breath, sun, body, seeds, bumble bee, insects.*' You stop: 'How many are there now?'

'Seven,' I say.

'Hm . . . *blood* . . .' you continue.

'Why you like blood?'

'I don't know. I feel blood is beautiful.'

'Really? But blood violence, and pain.'

'No. Not always. Blood gives you life. It makes you strong.' You speaking with surely voice.

You see things from such different perspective from me. I wonder if we change perspective one day.

'And why *breath*, then?'

'Because that's where everything is from and how everything starts.'

You are right.

'So, what else? Last favourite word?' I say.

'Suddenly.'

'*Suddenly*! Why you like *suddenly*? *Suddenly* not even noun.' You a strange brain, I think.

'I want learn most beautiful English words because you are beautiful'

'Well, I just like it,' you say. 'So what are your favorite ten words?'

I write down one by one:

'*Fear, belief, heart, root, challenge, fight, peace, misery, future, solitude . . .*'

'Why *solitude*?'

'Because a song from Louis Armstrong calling "Solitude". It is so beautiful.' I hear song in my ear now.

'Where did you hear that song?' you ask.

'On your shelfs. A CD, from Louis Armstrong.'

'Really? I didn't even know I had that CD.' You frown.

'Yes, is covering the dust, and look very old.'

'So, you've been through all my CDs?'

'Of course,' I say. 'I read your letters and diaries as well.'

'What?'

'And looked your photo.'

'What? You've looked through all my stuff?' You seeming like *suddenly* hear the alien from Mars attack the Earth.

'Not all. Parts that diary are make me sad. I can't sleep at night,' I say.

privacy

privacy n the state of being alone or undisturbed; freedom from interference or public attention

'YOU'VE INVADED MY privacy! You can't do that!' First time, you shout to me, like a lion.

'What privacy? But we living together! No privacy if we are lovers!'

'Of course there is! Everybody has privacy!'

But why people need privacy? Why privacy is important? In China, every family live together, grandparents, parents, daughter, son, and their relatives too. Eat together and share everything, talk about everything. Privacy make people lonely. Privacy make family fallen apart.

When I arguing about privacy, you just listen and not say anything. I know you disagree me, and you not want live inside of my life, because you a 'private' person. A private person doesn't share life.

'When I read your past, when I read those letters you wrote, I think you are *drifter*.'

'What do you mean by that?'

'You know what is drifter, do you? You come and leave, you not care about future.'

'To me, to live life is to live in the present.'

'OK, live in present, and which direction you leading then?'

'What are you talking about?'

'I mean, you don't have plan for tomorrow, for next year?'

'Well, we are talking about different things. I don't think you understand what I am saying. To me the future is about moving on, to some new place. I don't know where I am going. It's like I am riding a horse through the desert, and the horse just carries me somewhere, maybe with an oasis, but I don't know.'

Suddenly the air being frozen. Feeling cold. I not know what to say anymore. You older than me twenty years. You must understand life better than me?

You look at me and you say: 'It's like the way you came into my life. I feel as if I am not naked anymore.'

I feel as if I am not naked anymore. That a beautiful sentence.

I listen, I wait. I feel it something you not finish in your sentence, but you not want say it.

So I help you: 'Ok, I come into your life, but you not know if you wanting carry on this with me all the times.

You will want to break it and see what can make you move on . . .'

'We will see.' You stop me, and take me into your arms.

'It's important to be able to live with uncertainty.'

free world

free world esp. US historically non-Communist countries

You say:

'I feel incredibly lucky to be with you. We're going to have loads of exciting adventures together. Our first big adventure will be in west Wales. I'll show you the sea. I'll teach you to swim because it is shameful that a peasant girl cannot swim. I'll show you the dolphins in the sea, and the seals with their babies. I want you to experience the beauty of the peace and quiet in a Welsh cottage. I think you will love it there.'

You also say:

'Then I want to take you to Spain and France. I know that you'll love them. But we'll have to wait for a while. We need to earn some money. I'll have to get more work doing deliveries in the van to boring rich people. Can you put up with me being so boring – or do you think you'll get fed up with me after a while?'

Later you say:

'I feel so good about the love that you and I have with each other because it happened so quickly and spontaneously, like a forest fire.'

And you say:

'I just love the way you are.'

Everything good so far, but from one thing – you don't understand my visa limited situation. I am native Chinese from mainland of China. I am not of *free world*. And I only have student visa for a year here. I not able just leave London English language school and go live somewhere only have trees and sea, although is beautiful. And I can't travel to Spain and France just to fun – I need show these embassy officer my bank account to apply my Europe visa. And my bank statements is never qualify for them. You a free man of free world. I am not free, like you.

May

colony

colony n group of people who settle in a new country but remain under the rule of their homeland; territory occupied by a colony; group of people or animals of the same kind living together

THE WAY YOU make love with me, is totally new experience in my life. Is sex suppose be like this? Penetrating is way for you to enter into my soul. You are so strong. And your strength is overwhelming. For you, I am unprepared. You crush me and press me into your body. Love making is a torture. Love making is a battle. Then I get used it, and I am addicted by it. The way you hold my body is like holding small object, an apple, or a little animal. The force from your arms and your legs and your hip is like force from huge creature living in jungle. The vibrate from your muscle shakes my skins, the beating of your heart also beating my heart.

You are the commander.

You kiss my lips, my eyes, my cheek, my ears, my neck, and my silver necklace. It is like my necklace having a special magic on you. And that magic force you devote yourself to my body. Then you kiss my breasts and you suck them. You are like baby who is thirsty for mother's milk. You lick my belly and my legs and my feet. You possess my whole body. They are your farm. Then you come back to my garden. Your lips are wandering in my cave, and in that warm and wet nature you try find something precious, something you always dream about. You wander alone there and love there and want live there.

My whole body is your colony.

XIAOLU GUO is one of the best Chinese novelists of recent decades. When Xiaolu was born her parents gave her to a childless peasant couple in the mountains. Aged two, and suffering from malnutrition, they sent her to live with her illiterate grandparents in a fishing village on the East China Sea. This is where she grew up. She attended film school in Beijing and then, with a scholarship to study film, moved to Britain in 2002, knowing little more than a few English phrases.

A Concise Chinese-English Dictionary for Lovers, from which this Mini is taken, was written in English just a couple of years after Xiaolu moved to Britain. On her thirtieth birthday, Xiaolu decided to make her isolation in Britain, and her struggle with the English language, an asset and to write a novel about a Chinese immigrant. She kept a detailed diary, filled with the new vocabulary she learned, and this became the basis for the novel. The resulting book was shortlisted for the Orange Prize for Fiction. Xiaolu has written a dozen books in both Chinese and English and has directed a few award-winning fiction and documentary films.

RECOMMENDED BOOKS BY XIAOLU GUO:

A Concise Chinese-English Dictionary for Lovers
I Am China
Once Upon A Time in the East

Still talking about Language?

Babies
ANNE ENRIGHT

VINTAGE MINIS

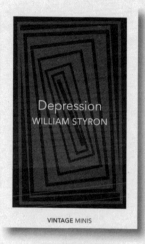

Depression
WILLIAM STYRON

VINTAGE MINIS

Race
TONI MORRISON

VINTAGE MINIS

Home
SALMAN RUSHDIE

VINTAGE MINIS

VINTAGE MINIS

The Vintage Minis bring you the world's greatest writers on the experiences that make us human. These stylish, entertaining little books explore the whole spectrum of life – from birth to death, and everything in between. Which means there's something here for everyone, whatever your story.

Desire	Haruki Murakami
Love	Jeanette Winterson
Babies	Anne Enright
Language	Xiaolu Guo
Motherhood	Helen Simpson
Fatherhood	Karl Ove Knausgaard
Summer	Laurie Lee
Jealousy	Marcel Proust
Sisters	Louisa May Alcott
Home	Salman Rushdie
Race	Toni Morrison
Liberty	Virginia Woolf
Swimming	Roger Deakin
Work	Joseph Heller
Depression	William Styron
Drinking	John Cheever
Eating	Nigella Lawson
Psychedelics	Aldous Huxley
Calm	Tim Parks
Death	Julian Barnes